THE
SWINGING
TREE

A SHORT STORY

RYNE GREEN

ISBN-13: 978-0-9982190-6-6

DEDICATION

To my mother, Danna

THE SWINGING TREE

Sarah Winkley never thought she would be back here, at her childhood home. She stood at the gravel road that led to the black pavement of the driveway, all of her luggage still in her 1990 Dodge minivan. This is where she would be living for a while, despite her mother's objections and the nagging question of what she was doing here repeating itself in her mind.

There was a lot of space from the neighboring house. In fact, her house was blocked off from others due to trees surrounding it, saved from the gravel road. It would be the perfect place to isolate oneself. When her mother took her away from the house at the age of 12, she loved the green scenery of the trees. They were the only good thing about where she lived. She had lost her love of the scenery over the years, now replaced with sad memories, but the isolation remained.

The house looked mostly the same since she had lived there, some 12 years ago. But there were signs of aging. The red bricks of the house seemed to have lost some of their color. Green stipes of paint were peeling off of the porch, and the rocking chair that stood there was covered in webs. The window that looked out to the front yard had a crack in it now, possibly from a rock.

If memory served her right, it was a rectangular shaped building with four bedrooms, a lounge, a living room, dining room and kitchen, all connected by one long hallway, and she doubted that much had changed. Connected to the building on its right side was a garage where her father kept his lawn mower, tools and other utilities.

The lawn all around the house was in desperate need of mowing, as the grass stood tall over her ankles. When she was a young girl, her mother warned her about walking in tall grass. She would tell her the story about how a childhood friend of hers stepped on a rattlesnake and had to go to the hospital. She doubted rattlesnakes were what she should worry about when walking in the grass. Bottles were scattered across the yard; her father never gave up on drinking and based on the broken syringes on the stone sidewalk to the porch, he picked up at least one new habit.

It was going to be an annoyance cleaning the mess her father had left behind. Her summer would be devoted to making this place livable.

Her father, Ted Winkley, had gone missing a little over a year ago. Since the divorce, the few he remained friends with said he became a hermit—maybe the woods around him had that effect. He would only go out into society for work or shopping, and nothing more. According to those who saw him last, he seemed nervous about something. Scared.

No one ever saw him again, but there were no signs of his leaving. His car was still parked in driveway, nothing seemed out of place, and nothing was even missing, besides him. His wallet was on his nightstand by the bed along with his phone. They searched the forest in case he might have been hurt during a hike but found nothing. Some suspect that he was in with the wrong crowd; others suggested he was abducted by aliens. In the end, no one could agree on what might've happened to him, but he was assumed dead shortly after.

If she were to guess, it would be that he was just some old, crazy man, fueled by alcohol and drugs, who left the house one night, got hurt and died. She wouldn't be surprised if they found his body over in another county, rotting with fungus and flies around his corpse. In truth, wherever he was, she didn't care.

Her mother didn't want her to move back here, and if it weren't for her money problems, she wouldn't have. She had no choice but to make do with it for the time being. Maybe if she made some repairs to it, she could sell it for a decent price and move somewhere closer to her college. But that would mean she had to put in the work for it to happen.

She walked to the garage, the kind with a door you had to lift up. She bent down and grabbed the handle. After a few tugs, she was worried that it was locked in place, but the last attempt proved successful.

Luckily, there was a lawnmower in the center of the room; in the back were his tools and a chainsaw. Along the wall, a weed-eater was hanging from a long nail. On the ground by the workbench was a tank of gas. At least she didn't have to pay for yard equipment, cutting down on her spending some. Just a couple of miles away was a supermarket that she and her mother would go for quick shopping. They should have the house supplies she'd need there. She made certain that it was still open on her way here and was pleasantly surprised it was.

She shut the garage door and returned to her

van to retrieve her luggage. She carried her belongings to the porch, setting down the first load. Before she went back to the car, something caught her eye and she smiled warmly. She made her way across the field of grass about 50 feet away to get a closer look.

It was a tree she remembered fondly. It was massive and round with thick branches. There was a split in the trunk that stretched up to the branches and all the way down to the base of the trunk, most likely from a lightning strike long ago. Parts of roots were protruding out of the ground. But what drew her attention to it was the swing hanging from the lowest branch. She looked at the trunk just left of the swing and saw it was still there: a carving of a heart with words inside right beside the large split that said...

Sarah and Tree
Friends Forever

Growing up, there were no children that lived close by to play with. No friends to go to for comfort when her parents' arguments were at their worst and became violent. The only harmony she could find was going to this tree. She would swing on it for as long as the arguments lasted, confiding in it her fears and dreams of something better. When she was out there, she did not hear the screaming and fighting anymore. It felt like she was safe from it all.

It was her own personal Giving Tree, but instead of apples and branches, it gave her comfort, peace of mind, and a friend. The night before her mother saved her from the house, she carved her declaration of friendship on the tree. She ran her hand across the tree's rough surface.

She was surprised that her father didn't cut it down after they left. He always complained about the tree, saying it was an eyesore. She suspected his hatred was the cause of her love for it. The previous owners of the house said that they didn't know how old the tree was, and that the swing was there before they came along.

She looked up at the tree branches. The five branches had smaller branches with leaves fully sprouted from them. The leaves were broad and blocked the sunlight from coming through, which cast shadows below it. It was a good place to sit down during the hot summer and relax.

She grabbed onto the rope to see if it was worn out. To her surprise, it wasn't. It felt as firm as the day she first touched it. She wondered if it could hold the weight of a grown woman. Without thinking, she tested it out, assuming the worst that could happen was a sore ass and dirty jeans. Once again, to her surprise, the ropes were strong enough to support her.

However, it felt awkward sitting so low to the ground as her knees curled upward, meeting her stomach. The swing board felt a little too small for her and much of her body was hanging off of it. Even if it could support her weight, it was still made for a smaller girl. Even still, it felt like she was 12 again, and even terrible memories have a few bright moments, too. She got off the swing and headed back, as she needed to look around the house to see all she had to do. Before leaving, though, she turned toward the tree and smiled.

"It's good to see you again," she said.

****

Sarah couldn't believe the state her father left the house in as she walked through the door. She was already expecting it to be filthy, but this far exceeded that. When she entered the house, she was greeted with a foul rotting smell as bad as a dumpster. She walked toward the kitchen where the smell was at its worst. Trash bins were overfilled with expired foods. Dishes were precariously stacked on top of each other in a sink filled with old water. There were pizza boxes on the counter that looked out into the living room, and there were bugs scattering across the floor.

She was almost awestruck by it all and even scared of what else she would come across next. Her father went missing over a year ago. No one had cleaned the place since, and she was dreading the work that she would be putting into this place. She walked into the living room to see if it fared any better.

The living room was a bit cleaner than the kitchen, but that wasn't saying much. There were plenty of bottles on the sofa counter and an ashtray with cigarette butts jutting out. There were tears in the sofa, and near the fireplace there was a tub of rotting logs and a basket with old newspapers in it.

Above the fireplace was a mantle holding several old picture frames of family members from her father's side. At the far end of the mantle was a couple of lighters and a bottle that still had liquid in it, probably whiskey, knowing her dad. She took it from the shelf and popped open the lid. She took a whiff and recoiled—it was definitely whiskey, and a strong one at that. She started coughing as she placed the bottle back where it was.

She saw all that she was going to see of the living room and was about to check the rest of the house, but once she turned to the hallway, she saw something and froze with anxiety. After 12 years, it was still hanging where her father had placed it. It brought back terrible memories, and she felt a pit growing in her stomach. It was a square, painted, wooden sign that showed a family of three all smiling and hands clasped, above them in bold letters read: **HOME IS WHERE MEMORIES ARE MADE**

She wondered if it was still there too and walked up to the sign. She gently lifted the sign up, and sure enough, there it was. A hole that the sign was meant to cover up. The last memory of her father was him putting that sign up. She never saw him again after that morning; her mother took her away while he was at work. The hole only reminded her of what had happened that night. She put her hand over her face, covering her nose and mouth, and for a moment, she felt that pain again. As if the flesh never forgot what it had felt.

She let down the sign to hide it once more. She had the sudden urge to leave the room. She walked out, but the memory lingered.

****

Sarah felt tired having explored the entire house, as if simply remembering was draining her energy. Since there was much to do in the days to come, she decided that it would be best to get some sleep. She finished washing her blankets and tidying the bed in her old room. It was surprisingly cleaner than the rest of the house. The only thing that she needed to do was dust it, but other than that it was fine.

Her father must not have spent much time in

his daughter's room since she had left, and it was better for it. When she was young, she never liked it when he entered her room without permission (or at all really). She just didn't like being in his presence and made it known, so her father didn't bother her often. It seemed like it was still something that her father respected even after they were gone. It was a small comfort that there were some things that her father didn't ruin for her.

Still, he did leave a huge mess for her to clean up. The bathroom floor and tub were stained, and the toilet had mold around it. It felt disgusting just being in there. Even the carpet of the hallway had stains and smelled of piss. It was going to take a lot of time for her to clean the house up, not to mention money. She wondered if she could clean the place up enough for someone to buy the place. Maybe someone would be interested in just buying the land from her. Their house wasn't much, but there was plenty of forest that someone could make good use of.

She imagined someone bulldozing their way through her house to make way for a new house and smiled. The thought of this place being torn down sounded rather appealing to her.

She turned off the lights and got under the covers. The room was as pitch black as the bottom of a cave. There weren't any post lights nearby to shed light into her room. As awful as the place was, the darkness was undisturbed and peaceful. When they left the house years ago, they moved to the city that was full of streetlights. It didn't matter what kind of shades they got, the light seeped through and kept her awake. The nighttime was the one thing that this rundown old house had over the apartment. It was easy to drift off to sleep.

Sarah wasn't sure if she was awake or still in a dream when she opened her eyes. She felt detached and dazed and peaceful. Yet she also felt like she was in control of her body, something she rarely ever felt while sleeping.

At her side, there was a faint tapping sound coming from her window. It was as if someone was hitting her window with something. A strange tapping sound that persisted as she weakly turned her head to the window. She realized that she couldn't see anything in the darkness but was too tired to get up. The tapping was faint and getting quieter, or perhaps sleep was drowning it out.

She felt pleasantly warm under the new comforter that she bought weeks ago. Her sleepy eyes began to close once more, deciding that this was all just a dream. As she drifted off into sleep, the tapping sound had faded away and she felt herself falling asleep again.

"Dear girl, is that you? Won't you come swing? I fixed it just for you. Come swing just like old times." Everything went dark once more.

Sarah spent more than she intended at the nearby supermarket. She bought supplies like air fresheners, mouse traps, garbage bags, bleach, dish soap, stain removers and more cleaning supplies, but also got some groceries for lunch, a cooler, a bag of ice, some soda, and water. It was always a dread to see how much such supplies would add up. Unlike food, clothing or movies, there was no excitement or fun to be gained from cleaning supplies. It only meant work.

At the register, she was surprised to see the cashier was the same woman who worked there when Sarah was a child. Back then, she was around 18, bright-eyed with a glow. Ten years later, wrinkles had begun forming, and strands of white shot out of her black hair like a sore thumb. The light that was once in her eyes had dulled and told of a lifetime of disappointment. A summertime employee that became full-time.

When she was ringing her up, she looked at her with a vague hint of familiarity. But she seemed to have forgotten her, or if she hadn't, she didn't care enough to ask. Sarah felt sad as she and her mother were regular shoppers there. Though it was probably easier to forget people when life hasn't been kind to you.

She headed back to the house and got to work on the yard. Before she could mow, she had to pick up all of the garbage. By the time she had finished, she had three bags full: mostly bottles (some filled with what she hoped was water that spilled on her), some needles, pizza boxes and other fast food bags. After picking it all up, she felt a soreness in her back.

Thankfully, her father's mower was a four-wheeler, so she got to sit while mowing the lawn. The hot noon sun was beating down on her, but at least she had the foresight to get the cooler and soda in advance. The motor roared as she rode down the lawn in a straight line before turning to repeat the process. The smell of gas rising from the mower was aggressive, but she stomached it. After mowing, she would have to weed eat around the swinging tree, as the thick roots made it hard to mow it.

It took a little over an hour to finish the yard,

and she felt some pride in her efficiency. The yard was covered in shredded grass, but at least it no longer looked like a miniature jungle filled with wildlife. The freshly cut grass scent was strong but pleasant. She parked the mower in the garage and grabbed the weed-eater. She still needed to trim those hard-to-reach places and decided to start with the swinging tree.

Instead of roaring like a beast, the weed-eater shrieked like a banshee, which only grew louder as it cut the grass. She was careful not to trip over the roots, slowly stepping over them and turning the weed-eater away from her on the side in case she did fall. She had been hit by one before and was not looking to repeat the experience. She passed the side with the swing and glanced at it.

What was meant as a glance turned into a stare as something was amiss about the swing. Was the swing seat higher off the ground now? It was now up to her waist, and the seat looked bigger than before, too. She placed her weed-eater on the ground and sat down on the seat. Her knees were no longer up to her stomach, and she could swing freely now. She swung for a moment and felt whimsical as she shot higher and higher up.

But as she began to think about it, an eerie, unsettling feeling took hold. How could the swing be like this now? Did someone fix it at night? She couldn't think of any other reason. But why would they do that? And *who*?

She remembered the dream she had last night. She couldn't remember much of it, but she was lying in bed and heard a tapping sound at her window. She began to wonder if that was actually a dream at all. She felt uneasy at the thought of someone coming to her house, which bought on other questions with it. Would they be back tonight? Would they try to get in? Were they old creepy friends of her dad? She started feeling pangs of anxiety in her chest.

She got off the swing and decided to hurry and finish weed-eating. She wanted to get inside the house as soon as possible. She grabbed the weed-eater and got back to work, but the thought persisted. She wondered if this mysterious person would come back tonight, what would she do then? Would they hurt her? She couldn't put it past anyone who would be friends with her father.

The day before, she came across a metal bat in her closet, a kid's baseball bat. Despite its shorter size, it would still hurt whoever was on its receiving end. So, it was decided that she would keep the bat next to her bed if the need were to arise.

****

Sarah looked at the digital clock on her nightstand: it was 12 o'clock now. She was tossing and turning in her bed, unable to fall asleep. Not because she was restless, far from it due to the day's work. It was that growing fear that planted itself earlier when she was on the swing, of someone coming to her house while she slept.

Why would someone come to her house? There was nothing here of much value. Were they after her? That wouldn't explain why they raised the swing up, even replacing the board. Why would they do that? There was no trace of anyone else being there. She couldn't even find the old board that they replaced.

She wondered how that was possible; there had

to be something left behind. After a second, she wondered if...maybe she just imagined the whole thing. This thought was strangely reassuring to her. Sure, it would be a problem in and of itself, but at least it meant that no one was coming to her house.

Still, she wished she wasn't alone in the house. It would certainly make her feel better about being there. She wished she could afford a dog, a friend to keep her company. A Rottweiler or German Shepherd would double as protection.

Her father would never allow animals into the house when she lived there. "It already costs too much to feed you," he would say. "Don't you make a big enough mess already?" It was bad enough that she didn't live close to anyone her own age, but she didn't get to keep a pet either. When her mom would dispute what he said, he would say he was just joking. He joked a lot back then.

She was deep in thought, remembering all the times she spent looking at the ceiling. As a child, it wasn't uncommon for her to hear shouting as she tried to sleep. The complete silence was actually something that took getting used to. When she lived in the town, there always a far-off sound, someone honking their horn or the train that drove through the town. She used to hate it, but now she longed for it to save her from this deafening silence.

Her eyes were adjusted to the dark and staring at the ceiling. Even though it was just her there, she anticipated her parents breaking out into argument at any moment.

She looked at the window and didn't see anything through the curtain. She decided to try sleeping again. She closed her eyes and felt more relaxed now, warming under her comforter and beginning to feel weary.

TAP…TAP…TAP… She heard a tapping sound that sent a jolt of alarm through her as she sat up in her bed. She looked at the window and saw something standing out there now, but wasn't sure what.

TAP! TAP! TAP! The tapping became louder as she sat in the bed, her heartbeat in sync with the sound. Someone came after all. She eyed the bat at the side of her bed and slowly pulled her blankets off and got on her feet. With bat in hand, she approached the window as the tapping became louder and faster. She grabbed the curtain, took a deep breath, pulled the curtain away and was greeted…by a tree.

She let out half a laugh of relief. It was just a tree, not some intruder. The wind must had been pushing the branches toward the window, and that's why it made that noise. She turned around and walked toward her bed, feeling silly about the whole thing. But she stopped in her tracks. Her blood ran cold when she realized something wasn't right. When she was a girl, she would often look out that very window and in all of those memories, there was one thing that was certain: there was no tree near her window.

"Dear girl, is that really you?"

She jumped and turned toward the window. She heard someone just talk, but no one was there. The voice sounded feminine, motherly even.

"Who said that?"

"It really is you! I never thought I'd see you again," the voice happily cheered, but there was still nothing. She looked at the tree and saw something on its trunk. It was her carving, and despite the dark, she recognized it.

"What the…" She stepped away from the window. It couldn't be, it wasn't close enough to her window for her to see it…She was in a dream, she had to be in a dream.

"Dear girl, I'm so happy to see you again! Look how much you've grown."

"What's going on here?" she slowly backed away. "WHO THE HELL IS THERE!?" She didn't know who she was yelling at.

"Dear girl, it's me. Don't you remember me? All those times we spent together." Although she could hear someone talking, she couldn't see anyone. All that she could see was-

"No…" she said, believing she must be crazy. "No, no, no, no, it can't be you."

"Yes, it is me!" it said. "We're back together again!" She heard the branches rattling and leaves fall to the earth.

"What the hell is this?" Sarah said. "This has to be a dream." She slapped herself on the side of her head. A sharp pain ran across her cheek, but it didn't wake her up. The slaps became increasingly more painful and frequent, but she still wouldn't wake.

"Dear girl, please don't hurt yourself," it said.

"What the hell is going on? I can't wake up," she said, rubbing her sore cheek. The pain felt too real for it to be a dream, but that couldn't be the case.

"You aren't dreaming. You have returned to me," it said.

"No, this is a dream! It has to be, I-I'm talking to a tree! This must be a dream." She was certain of this as sweat started to form on her forehead. It wasn't fear that she felt, but anxiety and uneasiness.

"It's okay, come out here," it said. "Swing on

my swing. Tell me your troubles just like the old days."

"No, I can't swing now," she said. Swinging was the furthest thing from her mind. "I'm not feeling well." She placed her hand on her forehead, thinking that she may be in a stubborn fever dream. She drifted off to sleep quicker than expected and would wake up. It made sense to her, but it didn't feel like it, and she could tell she didn't have a fever.

"Please, girl. Come swing on my swing. I fixed it just right for you. I thought I would never see you again after that day."

"I will swing tomorrow," she said without really paying any attention to what she was saying, like a mother holding their child's hand through a crowded sidewalk.

"No! It has to be now!" it pleaded. "I can't talk to you during the day."

"No, I can't. This isn't happening!" she said, backing herself toward the door, her hands desperately trying for the knob. Once she felt it, she quickly opened the door and rushed into the hallway but looked back to see that the tree was still there.

"Dear girl, please don't go! Please swing on my swing, dear girl." She shut the door. She couldn't hear it talking anymore, but she imagined it was trying to call out to her. Her heart was in her throat and her breathing was heavy. A cool cover of sweat spread across her brow. Did that really happen? Did the tree really talk to her?

It couldn't be, she knew better than that, but at the same time it felt so real. She didn't want to be near a window in case the tree spoke to her again. She made her way down the hallway, walked into the bathroom, and sat down on the toilet lid. It still had a faint smell, but it wasn't as bad as before. She sat there and began to doze off into sleep. Maybe the shock drained her of her energy, as she felt like fainting. Her last thoughts were about how this was all just a dream.

****

Was it all a dream? Sarah was certain that it was, yet it still felt like it happened. The sun was up, and the sky was blue. It was a particularly beautiful day, but it did not make Sarah feel better as she'd hoped. She was looking at the tree, but she stood at a distance from it. When she went out to look at the tree, she suddenly felt like she shouldn't get too close to it, as if it was a wild animal. An instinct that felt absurd since she knew it had to be a dream.

She checked where it had talked to her the night before, but nothing was out of place, no tracks—though she wasn't even certain what a tree track would look like—nor were there fallen twigs. Just some leaves scattered on the ground, but that could have been anything. The wind tended to carry leaves far away from the tree.

It felt strange that she was checking to see any sign that *a tree had walked to her window*. She wondered how a tree would move on its own, anyway. Would it pull its roots from the ground and use them as feet? Would the roots dig through the ground, pulling along the rest? Not that either happened since there was nothing there. She knew the only thing that made sense was she'd just dreamt the whole thing.

It was certainly preferable to other options, yet she remained unconvinced. It felt far too real to be imaginary. There was always a sneaking sense of detachment to her dreaming. A chilling possibility was that she was going crazy. A crazed murderer believes the voices in his head are too real to be fake, too.

When she woke up that morning, she found herself in the bathroom; in fact, the smell was the first to greet her. At first, she wasn't sure why she was in the bathroom, but quickly remembered the dream. She had planned on doing some work around the house, but the night before now took priority. She sat there and thought of any possible reason for her dream but couldn't think of anything. After a few minutes, she gave up on it and made her way outside to see if the tree was still there. A sense of foolishness lingered as she hesitated to take her first step off the porch. The dream got to her more than she could have excepted. That embarrassment stayed with her as she kept her distance.

As she looked at the tree, it did nothing. It didn't talk, didn't move, nothing. She tried to rationalize it by thinking that the dream happened because she was by herself there. She never did like being alone, and the woods caused her to feel isolated. It did when she was a little girl and was still doing it today.

As a child, there were times when she thought she had heard or seen things just out of the corner of her eye, usually at nighttime. Difference was, back then she had her mom and—as much as she hated to admit it—her dad to tell her that she was just hearing things. Now, it was just her, and that was the cause of the dream. It's what she told herself at least. That she just hearing and seeing things, even though she was a 24-year-old woman.

She looked at the tree yet again. It wasn't that she was afraid of going near it, but feared that if she did, it would be, in a way, admitting that she was taking this seriously. Giving a crazy dream the validation it didn't deserve. Still, it's not like she could just avoid the tree. She walked toward the tree but didn't dare venture any closer than 10 feet away. The shade of the tree covered her from the sun, and she called out to it.

"Hello…uh, can you speak?" she said, feeling more than a little ridiculous as she did, and even more so when the tree predictably didn't reply. It just stood there as a sudden breeze flew past and pushed the swing back. It swung back and forth until it's momentum slowly died off. As silly as it was, the breeze was like a wave of relief when the tree didn't respond. It was just a tree, after all.

It must have been a dream, period, she finally convinced herself. She tried to think about other times when she had lucid dreams like that one, to console herself, to remind herself that it happened from time to time. However, as she tried to remember, she realized there weren't any that felt this real. This one was different. Anxiety spread throughout her again as she looked at the tree.

"Maybe I should stay in Dad's room," she thought, albeit with some reluctance. She hadn't been in his room yet and imagining how filthy it must be was enough to make her gag. Still, she didn't think she had any other option now. She would have time to clean it up, no matter how dirty it was. But what if the tree came to his room? If she remembered correctly, her parents' former room did have a window, too.

"What the hell am I thinking?" She reprimanded herself for actually taking such things into consideration. It was just a tree, no different from any other tree on her property. No matter how much she tried to rationalize what had happened or repeated to herself that it was a dream, there was still uncertainty in her mind. There had to be a way to convince herself that this was all in her head.

That's when she had a thought, something that would prove if it was all a dream, a delusion, or something else entirely. She felt for her phone in her pocket and grabbed it. She looked at it for a moment and opened the camera app. She hadn't used it much but was certain she could take a decent enough picture with it.

If she were to have that dream again, she could just take a picture of it. A picture would prove that the tree wasn't there, that this was all just some crazy dream. Then she could go back to working on the house and leave this all behind her. She walked away from the tree since she needed to clean her Dad's room if she was going to sleep there for the night.

****

She assumed that her father's room would be messy like the rest, but it was much worse than she thought possible. She had never seen a bed so disgusting. The walls had stains on them for God knows how long. The carpet was covered with little black spots and fuzz that made her hesitant to step inside.

But it was enough work to make the time fly by, at least. It was nearing nine by the time she was finished, so she decided to go to bed. Another benefit of cleaning the room was that it took her mind off the tree. But she didn't forget, and it stood stubbornly in the back of her mind.

She placed her phone on the nightstand. She still believed that the whole thing was just a disturbing, uncanny dream, but the phone would confirm it. She got into the bed and closed her eyes. About 10 minutes later, she drifted off to sleep.

****

TAP…TAP…TAP…

Sarah opened her sleepy eyes to the sound of tapping. Was this a dream? There was a sense of déjà vu to it. She lifted herself out of bed and looked at the time on her phone: 12:00 A.M. If this was a dream, 12 seemed to be a recurring theme. Sarah gripped the phone in her hand and walked toward the window.

She felt calmer now than she did in the dream prior; knowing that something was a dream made things easier to go through, she supposed. She pulled the curtain toward the side and sure enough, the tree was there.

"Dear girl, I'm so glad to see you," the tree exclaimed. She could feel its excitement through the window, like a pet dog reuniting with a soldier coming home.

"Hello there," Sarah said calmly. Sarah figured she should just take the picture now, but decided to talk to it.

"Won't you come out here and swing on me like old times?"

"Actually, I wanted to ask you something," she replied. Even if it was a dream, it felt weird talking to a tree. It was what she used to do all of the time, only now the tree could carry a conversation. "You told me that you can only talk around this time. Why is that?"

"I don't know. I guess this is the time when I…wake up." An innocent enough answer, but it didn't tell her anything.

"How long have you been like this?" she asked.

"For as long as I remember. But why don't we talk about this outside? Talk to me like you used to."

"Wait, you said that you are awake at this time, so how can you remember me swinging on your swing? I don't ever remember coming out to see you at 12…" Was the tree trying to lie to her?

"I don't know why, but I just remember is all. I remember when you would come out here, but I couldn't talk to you."

"So why didn't you come to my window like you are now?" she asked. "You know where my room was after all."

"I…I was afraid that you would be scared."

"I see," Sarah replied. She lifted her phone up.

"What are you doing?" The camera went off.

"Well, now I will know if this is all real or not in the morning," Sarah said.

"What do you mean?" the tree asked, but Sarah just stared at her phone. The tree was in the picture, but she would truly know in the morning when she was certain she was awake. "Dear girl, please come swing on my swing again."

"Why do you keep saying that?" It seemed to be the only thing that the tree thought about, and it was getting on her nerves. She was panicking, and all it talked about was swinging on it.

"Because you haven't done that in such a long time, and I have been lonely since you left."

"Lonely, huh? Well, why not just talk to Dad when he was here?" she blurted out, but it did spark a realization. "Wait, do…do you know what happened to my dad?" It wasn't that she cared about her dad, but could it be possible that the tree knew something? It made her curious at the least.

"No, I don't know what happened to the awful man."

"Really? You never tried to talk to him? Never got him on your swing?"

"I could never let the awful man swing after all the horrible things he did to you!" It replied with a hint of disgust, a reaction that Sarah couldn't blame it for.

"Well, do you know anything that happened?"

"All I know is one night, he walked out, wobbling like he was about to fall over." Sarah assumed he must have been drunk. "He just disappeared into the shadows."

"That's it?" she said with disbelief. She supposed it was possible, but wouldn't someone have come across him eventually?

"Yes, he never came back. But I'm happy because you are here now!" the tree childishly cheered. "You can come swing and talk to me again. I don't have to be lonely anymore! And neither will you!"

This disturbed Sarah more than it should have. Mentioning her being lonely was unsettling, but in a way, almost comforting. Having someone who will listen to her here, not having to feel isolated anymore. It spoke to her on a level that she didn't like at all. Her mind kept telling her that it was just a tree.

"This has to be a dream." Sarah's back hit the wall and she sloped down. "Just one messed up dream."

"Why won't you talk to me anymore? You used to talk to me all the time! Like that last night before you left, do you remember what you told me then? What the awful man did to your mother? To you?" The tree didn't even need to ask if she remembered it. She remembered all too well.

****

Sarah was sitting on the couch in the living room, crying and covering her ears to block out the awful shouting between her parents in their room. Her father was mad because he couldn't find some of his money and accused her mom of stealing it. She didn't—he likely just misplaced it like he always had before. But that never stopped him in the past.

Sarah thought it was stupid that two people would fight over something like money. All of that screaming over a few dollars. However, her parents started screaming about everything now. That was how their fights always were, moving from subject to subject.

Her dad was now on his greatest hits: how her mom was raising her spoiled rotten because earlier that day, she was bouncing a tennis ball against the wall. "IF I HAD DONE THAT AT HER AGE, MY DAD WOULD HAVE BUSTED MY ASS FOR IT!"

"WELL I'M SORRY I'M NOT RAISING HER LIKE SOME CAVEMAN WOULD! MAYBE IF YOU ACTUALLY TREATED HER LIKE YOUR DAUGHTER INSTEAD OF SITTING IN FRONT OF THE TV ALL DAY, SHE WOULDN'T DO THAT!" This upset Sarah; she didn't know that bouncing her ball would make her dad so mad. She blamed herself for the argument. Sarah pressed her hands harder to her ears to block it all out. However, it was never enough. She could always hear their terrible shouting.

Her breathing became heavier, and her heart beat rapidly. She wanted to go to the tree, get on her swing and cry. She decided that she had listened to this for too long. But as she got up, she heard a loud banging sound. She recognized it as the door swinging open and hitting the wall. The sound of running footsteps rose from the hallway. Her blood went cold as she looked down it.

Her mom ran into the living room and fell to the ground. Her face was red and wet with tears, and blood ran down from her nose onto a busted lip. She turned and saw her standing there, and Sarah could see the fear in her eyes. She was on her hands and knees when her dad walked in. He wore a torn white tank top (they were called wife beaters for a reason), and his face was red with scorn in his eyes. His fat stomach hung out under his shirt, and his shadow cast over her mother.

"YOU THINK I'M A CAVEMAN, BITCH? I'LL SHOW YOU CAVEMAN!" he shouted in a devilish drawl as he balled his hand into a fist. With all of his strength, he threw his fist into the wall next to them with a loud cracking sound that made Sarah jump back in shock. There was a fist-sized hole in the wall now, with wood clips jutting out of it.

"I'M SORRY!" her mother cried. Sarah knew she wasn't, but just wanted it all to stop.

"YEAH YOU WILL BE!" He grabbed her arm and yanked her off of the ground.

"PLEASE STOP!" Sarah pleaded with him, but he just looked back with raging fires in his eyes. For all of her young life, her father had never shown any act of violence in front of her.

"YOU STAY THE FUCK OUT OF THIS IF YOU KNOW WHAT'S GOOD FOR YOU!" He shouted and grabbed her mother by the arm and gripped tightly. For whatever reason, Sarah decided to stop it. Something inside her told her that maybe she could calm her father down. She started moving toward them, failing to hold back her tears.

"It's okay, sweetie. Don't get involved," her mother pleaded, but Sarah didn't stop and grabbed at her father arm. Her nails dug into his arm and she looked up at him. All that looked back was a furious man, and he yanked his arm from her so hard she fell. "Please stop, Daddy." His face was still hot with rage.

"LOOK AT WHAT YOU DID!" he screamed at her, showing his arm to her. There were several red lines that ran down his arm. When he yanked his arm, her nails must have scratched him. "LOOK AT WHAT YOU FUCKING DID!" Sarah was horrified and backed away from him.

"I-I'm sorry!" she screamed.

"GODDAMNIT!" Her father balled his fist and swung, hitting her square in the face. She felt dizzy as she hit the floor with a hard bang to the back at her head. It felt like she was just hit with a sledge hammer and felt a pulsing pain spreading throughout her face. Her nose felt flattened. On the floor, she could taste something foul in her mouth and breathing through her nose felt wet with something.

"WHAT IS WRONG WITH YOU!" her mother screamed and sprinted to Sarah, holding her in her arms. Sarah put her opened hand on her nose and mouth and saw blood. She looked at her father who had just broken the only rule he ever seemed to abide. On his face was a look of disgust and sickness, as if the new low he had sunk to had taken a physical toll on him. "YOU FUCKING ANIMAL!" Her mother's face was resting on her head, and she felt the tears running from her eyes.

"THIS IS WHAT HAPPENS WHEN YOU GET INVOLVED!" her father shouted, trying to justify what had just happened. He walked over and Sarah braced herself when his shadow loomed over them. He grabbed her mother's arm and started ripping her away. Sarah didn't try to stop him this time as she sat there on the floor, her mind racing to make sense of it all.

Sarah sat there in horror as she heard her mother pleading with him, but he wasn't listening. He just complained about how unfair his life was, and how home was the one place he was supposed to be in charge. Once she heard the door slam, she thought the fighting would start again, but strangely it was silent. Sarah desperately prayed that the fight had abruptly ended, that her father came to his senses. Yet she heard footsteps heading toward the living room, and her father walked in.

She stood there wide-eyed and frozen with fear. For a moment, her heart stop beating, and time stood still. She feared she would receive another punch from the giant beast, but he stopped right at the hole he just created. She noticed something in his arms.

"Damn it, look at this hole. Maybe this will cover it." He spoke in an eerily calm voice as he hid the hole, as if all of that night didn't happen and he just came across the hole.

Even years later, she never understood why that remained such a clear image in her mind. Was it that he cared about the house more than the two of them? Did he somehow in his rage not realize that he was the one who did it? Or was he trying to pretend like the fight never happened and move on? When the sign was hung, her dad left the room, and shortly after, the screaming started anew. She looked at the sign that he had covered the hole with and in bold letters it read:

HOME IS WHERE MEMORIES ARE MADE

The horrible fighting continued, and Sarah felt terror like she never had before. Not just because of the fighting but knowing that there was nothing she could do about it. She felt trapped in this house and like she would never escape it. She eyed the phone stand on the counter next to the sofa. Long before this, her mother told her to never tell anyone about her father's treatment of her. She feared that the police would take her away. She wanted to stay with her mother, but it fed into that sense of powerlessness. Deep down inside, she knew that the only thing she could do now wasn't even going to help her mother.

With teary eyes, she ran outside, away from the screaming and fighting to the one friend she had. The one friend that would listen to her and would always be there for her. Once she hugged the tree, she got on the swing and began spilling her heart.

She swung on that swing for over an hour and began feeling a bit of relief. The tree had that sort of effect on her. When she swung high enough, it felt like she was flying away.

"You're my best friend, Tree." She got off the swing and headed toward the kitchen. Her parents were still fighting, but she didn't listen. Instead, she got a knife and hurried back outside.

She started carving something into the tree. "This is a sign of our friendship." It was a heart, and inside it, she carved:

Sarah and Tree
Friends Forever

****

"That was when you carved this symbol into to me. A sign of our friendship." It didn't need to remind her; she remembered it all too well. "But the night after that, you and your mother left me." The morning after that terrible night, Sarah's mother didn't take her to school. She figured it was because her nose looked really bad. But an hour or so after her father left, her mother came into her room and began packing her things.

Sarah didn't need to ask what she was doing. She didn't try to stop her, either. She wanted to leave the place as much as she did. There was a time that she expected that it was going to happen at any moment. With each argument, she thought it would be their last, and they would walk out that door. But it hadn't come, and she eventually gave up on that hope. When it finally happened, it felt like the best news she ever received. When they walked off the porch, she didn't turn back. Not even to look at the tree she spent so much time with. Getting away from her father was the number one priority.

"Why did you leave me?"

"That was when I was a kid and my mom knew she needed to get me out of here." She felt a pit in her throat, like she was about to cry. "I didn't need to come to you anymore."

"But you need me now," the tree said. "I can still feel all of your pain and loneliness!"

"I'm not lonely!" Sarah said.

"But you are...I can see it. Swing on my swing and you will feel better."

"SHUT UP!" she shouted at the tree. "I don't need to swing on you anymore." She turned and headed toward the door. All she needed was to take the picture, anyway. In the morning, she would finally see if this was all real or not. The tree pleaded with her to come back, but she ignored it.

The tears tried to force themselves out of her eyes and flow down her cheeks, but she held them back. The tree upset her more than she had expected. That's what happened when she thought about that night. Not just because of the fight, but because what the tree said was true. As crazy as it may sound, the tree was her best friend and after all of these years, that feeling seemed to still be there.

She was a grown woman now and still thought of a tree as a best friend. She thought that was just sad and was as lonely as ever. She made her way back to the bathroom since it was one of the only places that the tree couldn't talk to her.

She sat down on the toilet and began feeling sleepy once more. She wondered what she would do if the picture still showed the tree in the morning. It would mean that it was true, but it wasn't like she could tell anyone about it. They would think that she was crazy, and they might be right. She figured she could think about it tomorrow and drifted off to sleep.

****

The chainsaw was heavy in Sarah's hand as she stood feet away from the swinging tree. The gentle breeze pushed the swing into motion for a brief moment. Its shadow had cast over her as she stood there, troubled by what she had seen that morning. She wondered if she was really going crazy or this was all actually happening, or maybe both.

The answer only made things more unclear, though. She remembered looking at the picture from the night before. It was the same picture that she saw this morning, of a tree that shouldn't be there.

"What the hell is going on?" Sarah said in disbelief. When she saw the tree in that picture, she felt panic like she hadn't felt in years, if ever. Yet she wasn't sure if she knew what it meant. It just made her question herself and everything around her even more.

Was her crazy reserved for the night up to this point and just now leaking into the day? Or was the tree really coming to her window at night? She didn't like either possibility. It was at that moment she remembered the chainsaw that her dad kept in the garage.

If she sawed down the tree, then it couldn't come to her window anymore. Then she wouldn't have to think about it anymore. *"And then I will pretend none of this ever happened,"* she thought, believing she could live with that. She would not think about the swinging tree or her father anymore. They would both be gone, and she could finish all of the house work, sell it and leave for good.

"And I will never worry about it again," she thought, but now as she stood looking at the tree that had been her sole companion for so long, she began to waver. She thought about the things that it had told her. Did it

31

really miss her ever since she left the house? Was it really so glad that she had returned to the place? Did it really just want her to swing on it again? She nervously chuckled at the realization that she was even thinking about things most could never imagine.

She thought back to the past couple of nights and knew that this wasn't normal. She revved the chainsaw and it began to roar. She took a deep breath and stepped toward the tree. A part of her was concerned that the tree would pull its roots from the ground and try to run away.

Violent vibrations shook her as the chainsaw recoiled from the tree and she almost lost her grip. Her heart began to skyrocket from the surprise. She'd never held a chainsaw before and wasn't expecting this. She tightened her grip on the chainsaw and tried again.

This time the saw didn't bounce off of the tree, and she held the saw steadily as pieces of bark began flying in every direction. She would saw in a slanted angle so it fell away from her. The saw was slowly making its way, and nearly half of the saw was going through the trunk of the tree. The vibrations were still violent, and Sarah wanted to let go.

She took a break and turned off the saw, but her hands still shook as if she was still sawing her way through the tree. Her hands didn't quite hurt, but felt like her nerves were agitated. When she got back to sawing, her hands felt normal again.

An hour had passed, and she was close to getting to the other side. It would be over soon. As sawdust flowed through the air and clips of wood flung past her head, flashes of memories haunted her mind. Memories of when she was a young girl, swinging back and forth on the swing, trying not to think about her parents fighting inside. She looked at the carved message from years ago.

As sad as it may sound, she truly did still think of the tree as her friend. She wondered why she was going through with this? If the tree meant so much to her, then what was the harm of it talking to her? She looked at the tree and knew it was already too late to go back now.

Once it was done, the tree began to make a crackling noise and tilt downward. Just to be on the safe side, Sarah took a couple of steps back. The crackling noise grew louder as it fell to the ground. It made a loud booming sound when it hit the ground and she thought she felt the earth shake. Leaves were gently falling and its branches waved from the impact.

"It's done." Sarah stood there, staring at the tree. The agitated feelings in her hands had returned in full force, and they began to tremble. She took several deep breaths and felt like she was about to fall over herself. She steadied herself and surveyed the scene. The swing was on the ground now and just beyond it was the carved heart in its trunk. She looked around her yard, the house, and the woods and didn't hear anything beyond her own breath. She looked at the tree and realized something: if the tree didn't follow her to the window at night, then she would truly be all by herself.

"No," Sarah said, surprised by the tears forming in her eyes. She felt isolation grabbing hold of her once more. She realized that the tree was right about her being lonely. Now she had no one to talk to, and her swinging tree was gone.

She wobbled her way back to her house. She had done enough work on the house for one day. But once she got into the house, she fell to the floor and

covered her face with trembling hands, crying
for the friend that she had just killed.

****

**It was almost midnight now, but her remorse had
not diminished at all.** She just laid in her bedroom,
looking at the photo frame of her and the swinging tree.
It really was her own Giving Tree, and just like the boy
in the book, she abused their friendship. Her hands still
felt agitated from the chainsaw and only just stopped
trembling.

She wondered if the tree felt pain as she ran the
chainsaw through its core. She wondered if it was
screaming and because it wasn't midnight, she didn't
hear anything. She wiped away tears from her eyes.
Now that the tree was gone, memories of her asshole
father had returned. It seemed that the tree helped her
keep her mind off of the old man.

She looked at her phone. It was two minutes
until 12 now. She didn't feel tired at all and wondered
what she could do. She laid flat on her bed and stared at
the ceiling. Time felt frozen. She could hear the
screaming from the past fill the house. It was her
father's violent screams and her mother's pitiful
begging for mercy.

Her father was now a figment of her past, with
no point in thinking about him. But the swinging tree
was gone, so she supposed she shouldn't think of it
either. She got off of her bed to head to the kitchen to
get something to eat. Something to take her mind off of
things. She grabbed the door knob and began to turn it.

TAP…TAP…TAP…TAP…Sarah's heart
skipped a beat when she heard it. She slowly turned

around and saw it there.

"Dear girl."

"You're...alive?" She felt a mix of delight and shock. "But how?"

"Dear girl, why did you do that to me? It hurt so much."

"I... I..."

"Do I not matter to you? Do you want me to go away?"

"No!" Sarah tearfully said and stepped toward the window. She got onto her knees and pressed her face against the window. "No, I don't want you to leave. I'm sorry."

"But why did you do that to me?"

"I don't know." Sarah said. "I thought I was going crazy. I thought it was the only way."

"But do you regret it now?"

"Yes. After I did it, I realized you are the only true friend I ever had." She tried to catch her breath. "I thought it wasn't normal that I was talking to a tree."

"But you talked to me all the time when you were a little girl. Only difference is now I can talk back to you."

"You're right." Sarah realized she didn't have to be alone in this place anymore.

"Then come out here, dear girl. Come out here and swing on my swing."

"Just like the old days," Sarah smiled. "Okay, I will be right out there."

"You know where I'll be."

Sarah got off of the ground and started running toward the door. She had a second chance and wasn't going to ruin it this time. She got to the door in the hallway and grabbed the knob, but first noticed a switchblade on the counter near her. She put it in her pocket. She would make a new sign of their friendship like she did long ago. She was certain that the tree would love it.

She pushed open the door and ran out into the starry night sky.

****

Sarah was so excited to swing on the tree that everything else became a blur to her as she ran toward it. It was there like it always had been, waiting for her. She got on the swing and began shifting back and forth to gain momentum. Soon her feet were off the ground, and she felt like a child again. The moon shined brightly, and she could see far out into the distance.

"It's been so long hasn't it?" Sarah said to the tree.

"Indeed, it has."

"But how did you get back up?"

"I don't know how, but your father did the same thing."

"He did?" Sarah said in surprise.

"Yes, for some reason my roots grow back into the ground. I don't know how it happens." Sarah just smiled.

"I see," Sarah said. "I'm just glad that we're back together."

"I am too, dear girl. I don't think we will ever be apart again."

Sarah agreed. She found herself higher than she had even been before. She opened her eyes again and saw something. Something she was never aware of before. But before she could get a clear look, the swing was going down again. The shadows covered it, yet she thought something was staring at her. She swung back up to get a better look of the thing but then—

"What th-" Sarah let out as the swing seat under her fell apart and she fell to the ground, landing on her hip. A sharp pain coursed through her. Did the swing suddenly break?

"Are you okay?" the tree asked.

"Yeah. I guess the swing just bro-" Before she could finish, she felt something wrap itself around her neck. She was immediately hurled upward off the ground. Whatever was around her neck started to tighten until she wasn't able to breathe.

She reached around her neck to see what it was that held her. It felt like a rope, a noose. She looked around frantically to see what was going on, but she just flailed around as she went higher up. Panic and confusion set in as the tree began to talk.

"Finally. I've waited so long for this moment." Sarah couldn't say anything but realized that she was rising higher up toward the tree. "You weren't ripe when you first swung on me."

Sarah wanted to ask what it was talking about, but only grunts came out,

"But now, you are just ripe." As her lungs began to burn, she realized that it was the tree that was hanging her.

"Wha-"

"When you left, I thought I had lost my chance forever. But now you are here."

Sarah heard a loud crackling, splitting sound coming from the trunk. Sarah turned her head enough to see the long split in the tree was now a mouth opening up. The moonlight shined on something in the tree, and her eyes shot open in disbelief. Headless bodies were stacked on top of each other, stuffed in the trunk. She could tell that some of the bodies were rotten and must had been in the trunk for decades, maybe even longer.

Their foul odor and the strong scent of blood wafted toward her, and had her eyes not been watery already, they would have then. How long had those bodies been stuffed into the tree? Before she and her family moved into the house? Questions spiraled in her mind, but her focus was on the headless bodies in the tree and the rope around her neck. Where were their heads? She remembered the thing that caught her eyes before falling off of the swing. She swung her body around and saw it hanging. It wasn't a fruit; *it was a head.*

That was when she noticed that it wasn't the only one, as many other heads were dangling from nooses wrapped tightly under foreheads. Some of the heads look rotten and dead. But she could see their eyes looking and turning about in their heads, some opening and closing gaping mouths. Were the heads still alive? How could that be possible? How hadn't she or anyone else noticed them before? Was this some trick by the tree?

"You will be one of my prettiest fruits. Much prettier than him."

Sarah knew immediately what it meant by this, as her sight returned to the first head that caught her attention. Unlike the others, this head stared back at her with a look of horror and disbelief. She never thought she would had to see those eyes again. Not too far from her, hanging from the same thick branch was her father's head.

"You should have seen him that night," the tree said in a different tone. The head was moving his mouth as if it was trying to tell her something. The sight of his head was repulsive to her. "He came out of the house, drunk as usual, when he walked over to my swing and sat down! He was such an awful man, and I didn't want him on my swing. But as he swung and cried, I felt anger like I never had before. I always wanted to make you one of my fruits, but he ruined it all, so I decided to take his head instead."

Sarah struggled to free herself from the noose, but couldn't break free of it. Her throat burned as the rope grew tighter and tighter. "Right as my vine wrapped around his fat neck, he screamed for forgiveness and how he was sorry. No one answered his calls as I lifted him up." Her heart was beating rapidly in her throat and fear was coursing through her. Was what happened to her father going to happen to her? Would her head be hanging next to her father's for the rest of time, those below completely unaware of their presence? Even if she were dead, she couldn't stand the thought of being near him.

The thought made her even more panicked and desperate to escape her noose, but the more she struggled, the tighter it became.

"Don't fight it, the pain will be over soon. We can be together forever now. You will never be lonely again." She couldn't tell if the tree was mocking her or if it was being sincere. Tears were running down her cheeks and her lungs were burning. The vines rubbed at her neck and strung her. She couldn't get her fingers under the vines to pull them off. Her body felt like it was being drained of its strength and energy. She realized that this was it for her. This was how she was going to die. She looked at the trunk of the tree and noticed next to the opening in its trunk was the carving that she put into the tree so long ago.

A new feeling sank into her, one of betrayal. Perhaps she couldn't blame the tree since she tried to saw it down. She wondered if that had anything to do with this, or if this was always its plan. She remembered the joy she felt when she ran out to the tree. She was so happy that she was even going to…

That was when she remembered the switchblade in her pocket. She ripped her hands off of the rope, running more on instinct than brain. She felt the knife in her pocket and the urge to live had returned. She grabbed the knife and opened it up. She wasn't sure if it would cut through the rope, but she had to try. She started slashing at the rope behind her head. Her vision began to blur, and her face was covered in tears. She felt her eyes getting heavy as she suffocated, running on fumes now. She kept cutting at the vines. Her vision was starting to dim, and she felt weightless, knowing that it was too late for her. However, that weightlessness only lasted for a few seconds before she felt herself falling down to the ground.

She hit the ground and a jolt of pain drove through her. But she didn't care as she realized she could breathe again. Her sight came back, and she was on the ground now. She didn't notice the stinging pain around her neck as she drank in the air that never tasted so sweet before.

"NO!" the tree screeched in anger, and she turned to it in fear. She started backing away from the tree.

"YOU…. YOU…. YOU….!" She tried to say it

was trying to kill her, but couldn't form the words and crawled back from it like a crab, pointing her finger at it. The ropes that used to be a swing started reaching out to her as if the vines were stretching themselves. "Just what the hell are you?" Sarah said as she got off the ground, breathing heavily as she felt the rope burn from the noose. The vines stopped after about 30 feet and couldn't extend anymore.

"NONONONONONONONONONO!" the tree howled. "I have waited so long for this moment." Sarah still couldn't believe what was happening. "YOU WILL BE MINE!" The tree began violently shaking itself around, its trunk twisting and turning like a snake, and the ground beneath it was tearing apart.

Sarah just watched, wondering what it was trying to do, but realized it had done the same the last two nights. The tree roots ripped themselves out of the ground and wiggled, feeling the ground around them. She eyed her house and knew she could make it there and wait until the daytime. However, the tree freed itself from the ground and its roots carried it toward her. It resembled an earthbound octopus using its tentacles to cross land, but the tree moved much faster than expected.

The way the tree moved was so disturbing that it gave her pause and she couldn't help but stare. But as it got closer to her, she snapped out of it. She ran toward the house, which only took seconds but felt like an hour. She glanced behind and was surprised by how the tree was catching up to her and how close its noose made of vines were to her. There were even more vines now.

She jumped onto the porch and grabbed the doorknob, her heart beating faster than it ever had before. She opened the door and as she let go of the knob, she felt a sharp whip from one of the tree vines. She recoiled and held her hand in the other, nursing the new red mark across her hand. Those vines were made of tough material and were just as dangerous as whips as they were nooses.

"GET BACK HERE, DEAR GIRL!" Sarah ran inside and shut the door. As she let go of the knob, the door was ripped off of it hinges. Sarah jumped back with a scream, shocked by how strong the tree was as it flung the door to the side. A noose shot out at her. She ducked away from it but was hit by another one that wrapped around her shoe.

"GET OFF OF ME!" Sarah shouted, but the tree began pulling her outside.

"I'M NOT WAITING ANYMORE!" Sarah tried to pull back, but the tree was too strong. She thought to use the knife to cut through the vines, but she didn't have it anymore. She must have dropped it during her fall. As the tree pulled her closer, she realized that her shoe was coming off, so she slipped her foot out of the shoe and backed away into the hallway. She didn't know what she could do, but she was out of its grasp for now.

She looked toward the door, half expecting the tree to try and force itself through, but it didn't. It just stood by the porch with it vines entering the house again. Sarah thought she would be okay if she was out of the tree's sight, so she ran toward the bathroom and closed the door. She stepped into the tub and was silent, hoping the tree couldn't tell where it was. She heard the vines banging on the walls of the hallway, like it was trying to feel for her.

TAP…TAP…There was a knocking on the

bathroom door, and Sarah's heart jumped into her throat. The vines ran along the door, trying to find a way in. She was silently panicking, wondering what she could do? What if it ripped the bathroom door out? She would have to go to another room, but each of the rooms had a window in it. It wouldn't have any trouble going through the window.

How could she stop the tree? Was there any way to stop it? She had sawed it down earlier, but it got right back up. Was there no way to beat it? Since sawing didn't work, maybe setting it on fire would. But she didn't have any matches or a lighter on her, not to mention that the tree wouldn't just stand there and let her start the fire. But that made her remember something and she got out of the tub. She tiptoed mostly out of fear that the vines could hear her. The tree was capable of things she didn't think possible, so she wasn't taking any chances. She tiptoed to the sink and knelt down. She opened the cabinet door, and there it was: a package of paper towels that she had bought was sitting there.

She took about 10 folds of them, figuring it would be enough, and looked at the door. The vines were still feeling the door and if she opened it, then it would know she was there. But if her plan was going to work, she would have to go to the living room right at the end of the hallway. If memory served her right, what she needed was waiting on the shelf above the fireplace.

She knew that she would have to run past the tree to get to the living room. That would be a risk. She would also only have one shot at it. She took a deep breath, mustered up what courage she had left, and placed her hand on the door knob. She would open the door on the count of three.

"One..." she whispered to herself. "Two..." She took in a final breath and could hear the vines banging on the walls. She thought of her mother and how she wished she would have listened to her. Tears ran down her cheeks, mostly out of fear. "THREE!" She opened the door and saw the vine there in front of her. She ran past the vine as it shot at her and missed. She ducked under it and continued to run as the vine tried to wrap itself around her.

Fortunately, the hallway was narrow, so the tree had to pull its vine back to the door entrance. Soon she would have to pass it, and the tree would be waiting for her with vines ready. Past that was the living room. So, without stopping, she ran past the tree.

"Won't you come here, dear girl?" the tree asked, as if it thought that would convince her, but shot out its vines toward her once more. Sarah ducked out of the way of the first vine but was hit on the arm by the second one.

"ARGH!" She yelped in pain, even while bracing for it, and she lost her balance and fell to the ground. Luckily, the fall proved helpful since the vine didn't wrap around her.

"COME HERE!" It pulled back its vines and shot them at her again. Sarah kicked herself off the ground, barely dodging the vines, and finally made it to the living room. She quickly scanned the room and saw it on the shelf above. Sarah hurried to the shelf and grabbed the bottle. It was the one that she came across on her first day there. For the first time, her father's drinking problem would actually help her. She opened its lid and took the paper towels from her back pocket. She stuffed the paper towel in the bottle until there was just enough sticking out of it. She tilted the bottle so the towel would soak up some of the liquor; that's what she thought she was supposed to do, anyway. Admittedly, this was her first Molotov cocktail.

The vines of the tree entered the living room and waved around, trying to find her. Sarah looked toward the end of the shelf and saw the lighter lying there again. She'd only seen this in movies. But it was her only hope of getting out of this alive. Sarah ran toward the lighter, avoiding the vines as they came too close. She reached out to the lighter and grabbed it.

It was one of those old lighters that required you to turn a flint wheel to get it to started. She placed her thumb on the rough flint wheel and pressed down on it. Nothing, not even a spark. Sarah felt her heart sink deep into a void as she kept turning the wheel.

"C'MON! You've gotta be shitting me!" Sarah panicked as she frantically tried to start the lighter. So much so that she didn't feel the vine wrap around her leg. "WHOA!" She fell to the ground with the bottle still in her hand.

BANG! The bottle made a loud sound as it slammed against the floor. She felt the vine tugging her into the hallway. She wanted to scream but fought her nerves to remain calm.

She looked at the bottle and felt relief that it hadn't shattered yet. There was a big crack in it and looked like it would shatter if it hit something hard enough. Perfect for her intentions, but something was wrong…where was the lighter?

Sarah looked around and found the lighter within her reach on the floor. She reached out to grab it, but was dragged away. It was getting further and further away. She tried to grab it again, but it was just out of reach. Everything felt like it was in slow motion as she tried to grab it, and her breathing became heavier. That lighter was the only hope she had; if she couldn't reach it, she might as well give up any hope.

"ARGH!" She made a last ditch push toward it. She almost let out a laugh of relief when she felt it in her hand and tightened her grip on it. The pull from the tree brought her back to reality though. She held the lighter and bottle close in front of her as she tried to start up the lighter.

She tried flicking on the lighter, but no flame came out of it, just a spark. She was at the corner of the hallway that looked out to the doorway. She only had a few mere moments left before it was all over

"It's only a matter of seconds now, dear girl." It's as if it knew what was going through Sarah's mind. It was tugging harder on her now, dragging her faster, and not going to wait anymore. Tears were running down Sarah's cheeks now as she started losing hope that she would survive this. She thought of her mother being dragged down this hallway and wondered if she felt the same. An urge to scream for it all to stop. She was halfway out of the door and onto the porch. Her thumb felt sore from turning the flint wheel and strung a little as she pressed down on the wheel. She looked at the tree and as it loomed over her, she felt like a little girl on the night her father looked down at her.

She froze up reliving that moment once again. The vines pulled her out onto the porch now that she wasn't resisting.

"That's right, just let it happen," the tree said calmly. "You will be at peace, just like him." Sarah looked up at the branches and saw her father's head hanging from it. Seeing it dangling from the tree was a pathetic sight. The thought of her head hanging from the same tree was a revolting thought.

"*SNAP OUT OF IT!*" her inside voice shouted. She couldn't give up now; she was going to survive this. She survived that night all of those years ago, and in the morning, she left. She would survive this night, and in the morning, she would leave it again. With that, she pushed down on the flint wheel…an orange blazing light appeared before her, the most beautiful thing she had seen in so long.

Sarah lifted the paper towel sticking out of the bottle to the small flame; luckily, the tree hadn't noticed. Smoke began to float up from the paper towel and the fire spread to the towel. She was just feet away from the tree and she lifted her head off of the ground. *"It shouldn't be hard to hit it from here."*

She gripped tightly to the bottle, felt the warmth from the growing fire that was on the paper towels. "It's almost time," the tree said with glee. Not saying a word, Sarah threw the self-made explosive at the tree with all of her strength. This was the moment of truth. The bottle shattered as the flames spread across the tree.

"AAAAAAAAAAAAHHHHHHHHHHHHHHH HHHHHHHH!!!!"

The tree backed away from the porch, and the vine wrapped around Sarah's leg loosened enough for Sarah to get out of it. She backed herself away from the tree until her back was at the wall and watched the tree writhe in what seemed like pain. The flames spread more rapidly than she had expected. What had started out as a flame on paper towels now was a flaming orange inferno.

She could feel the warmth from the glowing

flames. Its light cast onto the several heads that still hung from its branches. Their eyes looked like they were in pain.

"AAAAARRRRRRGGGGGGGGGHHHHHHHHHHHH!" the heads began screaming, almost giving Sarah a heart attack. It seemed like the heads were still alive. Or it was just another trick of the tree. She just sat there on the porch, staring at her father's screaming head.

As a child, she had hated the man, something that didn't change during adulthood, yet she couldn't help but feel a little bad for him. Did even a wife-beating piece of shit deserve to go through...*that*? She thought about the last time she had seen him, when he put up that sign over that hole. Hiding the hole, hiding the ugly truth... like a swing hiding a tree's true nature. Her father's head started fading away into ashes and the other heads followed suit. She wasn't sure what it meant, but she liked to think that they were free. Free of what, she didn't know.

She saw the heart that she had carved into the tree that said that they would be friends forever. She breathed deeply, and relief washed over her, but there was something else, too. She knew she had to do what she did, but she couldn't shake her undeniable sense of sorrow, too. Even after what it tried to do, she supposed there was still a small part of it that felt like her friend. Despite its intentions, it was still the one thing that she could go to for some comfort.

Suddenly, the flames on the tree went out and the tree just stood there. Sarah worried that it was still alive and picked herself up, preparing for a second round with the tree. However, with a gentle breeze, the tree blew away as ashes until it was no more. She watched the ashes float away into the shadows and felt certain that it was finally over. She stepped off of the porch, walked onto the yard, looked out on the field, and saw nothing was there anymore.

She saw the torn ground in the earth where the tree used to stand, giving her a sense of relief. It felt like any doubt she still had up to this point had finally gone away. All that happened had actually happened. That's how she saw it anyway. She looked back and decided it was time for her to leave the place for good.

****

Sarah's minivan was starting to act up as she pulled into the gravel road that led to her childhood home. Maybe she would have to use some of her house money on buying a nice used car. A Malibu maybe; anything but a minivan would do, though. Fall was almost here, and the leaves were starting to change color.

Her college semester would be starting again soon, and she decided to study child psychology. After everything she'd been through, she felt like she was meant to help other children struggling through hard times. The courses for it would be pretty expensive, though, and she doubted that the money from the house would cover it. Still, she wanted to do it and felt like children needed someone to tell their worries to.

She made it to the parking place at the house and saw a black Dodge waiting for her. Once she got out of the car, a man and woman in their 30s got out, while the two girls in the back remained seated, focused on their phones. The Madison Family had bought the house from her. They were tired of the city life and wanted to live somewhere quieter. The father greeted her with a smile and shook her hand.

"Ms. Winkley, right?" he asked, and she nodded her head. The mother walked up to them with a smile that could light up a cave.

"We can't say just how glad we are to have found your house. We know we are going to love it here."

"Yeah, I think you will," Sarah said, and she meant it. Something about them seemed like they were made for a more rural lifestyle.

"Anyway, you did a great job fixing up the place."

"Yeah, it took a couple of months of hard work, but I got it done," Sarah said, feeling like the work was finally worth it now. "Anyway, here is the last key to your new house." Sarah handed the key to them, the same key that was given to her earlier this year.

"Oh, before you go, there is something you forgot," the woman said and hurried into the house. Sarah didn't know what she was talking about and stood there to see what it could be.

"So, where have you been staying at these past couple of weeks?" the father asked, trying to strike up a conversation.

"Oh, my mom is helping me pay for rent at my college campus," Sarah said, though she left out how small it was. Certainly not as big as her bedroom here, and she couldn't bring much with her. Still, she was happy to finally be leaving this place. She never should have set foot back in it, and after today, she never planned to look back on it. Not just because of the tree, but because there was nothing but bad memories here. The mother walked out of the house and hurried back to them. Sarah recognized the thing she was holding in her arms.

"You must have forgotten about this."

"Oh yeah…this." Sarah forced a smile. She fixed the hole under it, but never did like looking at it and considered it a gift of sort to the new homeowners… just one that they wouldn't know about until she was gone. "Thanks."

"It seemed strange that you put it in such a place though."

"Oh, I guess that's just my father for ya." She never told them about what had happened there. She doubted anyone buying a new house would want to know that bit of history. "Well, it looks like you will have a lot of unloading to do."

"Yeah, the storage truck should be here soon," the father said.

"I better let you get to it then," Sarah smiled and shook both of their hands once more. "You all enjoy the house, okay?"

"Take care and good luck with college." With that, she headed back to her van and got in. She tossed the sign on the passenger seat and began driving down the gravel road one last time. She felt relief, knowing that it was finally over as she was about to pull out onto the road, but hit the brakes. She noticed an opened garbage can at the side of the road, next to the mailbox. She looked at the sign and rolled down the window. She picked the sign up and threw it out the window into the garage can.

"No board," she said, getting a strange sense of wholeness from it. She pulled onto the road and started driving away, never looking back.

"Abby, c'mon! We got to get the stuff inside," her mother told her as she sat on the porch, still focused on her phone.

"I will in a second," Abby replied, wanting to put it off as long as possible. She was still mad that they would be moving into the old house in the first place. Why couldn't they just stay in the town? The woman they bought the house from seemed excited to leave the place.

"Hey, is it okay if we look around the place?" her little sister Missy asked.

"Sure, go ahead," their father said. "I'm sure you are going to love it." The young girl ran around the corner of the house. Abby just sat there.

"You know you'll have to give this place a chance," her mother said. "So why not look around?"

"Hmpf!" was all Abby let out. She really wished they would just go back to their old home where all of her friends were at.

"WHOA! Look at this!" her sister screamed with excitement. Her father and mother ran around the corner. Abby sat there for a moment but decided to see what the big deal was. She got up and walked to the back where the rest of her family stood, looking up at a great old tree.

Abby look at the tree and its detail became clearer. A large split ran down the trunk of the tree. She walked next to her mother and saw a swing hanging from it. Parts of the roots were protruding from the ground.

"Look at this tree," her mother said in awe.

"I know, but where did it come from?" her

father asked.

"What do you mean?"

"When I was looking at this place, I don't remember seeing a tree here." Abby looked at her father who had a confused look. However, her sister got on the swing and started pushing her weight back and forth.

"Missy, get off of that," her mother said. "The swing might fall apart."

"C'mon, push me higher!" However, they could hear the moving truck pulling into the driveway.

"Maybe later," her father said. "We've got to go unpack." The little girl jumped off of the swing and walked with her father and mother, hand in hand. Abby just stood there for a moment and looked at the tree. She wasn't sure why, but there was something about the tree that just stood out. She looked at the base of the trunk and noticed a craving of a heart in it. There was something written into it too.

Sarah and Tree
Friends Forever

Sarah was the name of that woman who was just here, Abby thought and chuckled.

"Being friends with a tree? That's just sad." She smirked and started heading toward the moving truck.

"Dear girl…" She jumped in surprise at the sound. She turned back to the tree but saw nobody there, only the tree.

"ABBY, C'MON!" her mother shouted.

"Urgh…. OKAY! BE RIGHT THERE!" She turned and headed back to her mother. The tree just sat there…waiting for someone to swing on its swing.

ABOUT THE AUTHOR

Ryne Green is an author living in Paintsville, KY. His previous book was titled *A Baby Cries*. In addition to writing, he spends his days gaming and spending time with his niece Natalie and his beloved dog Cooper.